My Wicked Stepmother

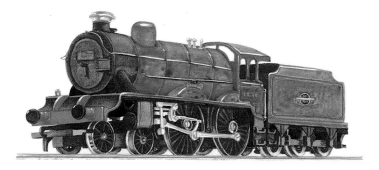

NORMAN LEACH

with pictures by JANE BROWNE

Julia MacRae Books

LONDON SYDNEY AUCKLAND JOHANNESBURG

My name is Tom. I live with my dad.
We were happy together. . .

First published in Great Britain 1992
by Julia MacRae
an imprint of Random House
20 Vauxhall Bridge Road, London SW1V 2SA

Random House Australia (Pty) Ltd
20 Alfred Street, Milsons Point, Sydney, NSW 2061, Australia

Random House New Zealand Ltd
18 Poland Road, Glenfield, Auckland 10, New Zealand

Random House South Africa (Pty) Ltd
PO Box 337, Bergvlei 2012, South Africa

Printed in China

Reprinted 1993

British Library Cataloguing in Publication Data is available

ISBN 1·85681·113·1

But now I have a wicked stepmother.
She is a witch. I hate her. My dad thinks he loves her.
She put a spell on him and he thinks she is young and beautiful, but
I know she is middle-aged and ugly and a horrible witch.

I've got a new Robin Hood outfit from my dad.
Green tunic and hat and bow and arrow.

I went to show my friend Jack.
He said, "So what? I got one of
those last year."

I went to show my friend David. He said,
"Bows and arrows are boring!
I've got a laser gun."

I felt fed up. I went back home.
The wicked stepmother said, "Tom, you look great
in that Robin Hood suit. Let me see you shoot
your bow and arrow."

But I didn't, because I'm not nice to wicked stepmothers.

My dad gave me a Superman cape made with real silk! I put it on.

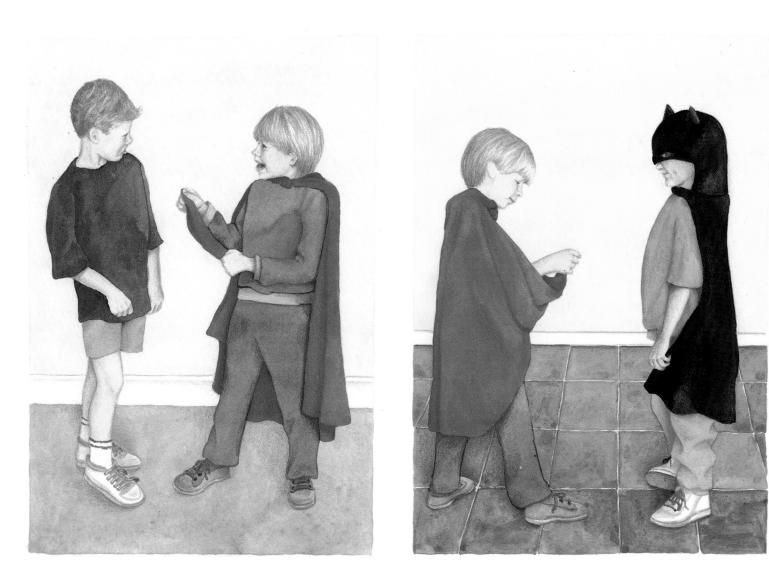

I went to show my friend David.
He said, "So what! I got one of
those last year!"

I went to show my friend Jack.
He said, "Superman's boring!
I've got a Batman cape."

I went back home.
My wicked stepmother said, "Hey look! It's Superman,
come to rescue us from danger!"
I almost smiled at her but I didn't because she's my wicked
stepmother and I don't smile at wicked stepmothers.

I don't tell her what I think of her or she might turn me into a frog.

It was my birthday. Jack and David came to tea.
But in pass-the-parcel Jack cheated, and when we played musical
chairs, David pushed me off and I got cross and cried a lot.

Then the wicked stepmother

brought in the cake and it was like

a cat and had seven candles and I

lit them and took a deep breath.

But before I could blow them out,
Jack and David blew them out.
I was angry and burst into tears.

The wicked stepmother said to David and Jack,
"If you do that again I'll turn you into nasty little toads!"

She lit the candles again and I blew them out all in one go.

And then we had presents and David gave me a toy car, and Jack gave me a toy car. Dad gave me two books and a tape and some new pyjamas.

The wicked stepmother gave me a toy train set, which was what I really wanted. It was my favourite present, but I didn't play with it because it was bewitched.

Then my dad came home from work and David's mum and Jack's dad came to collect them, and me and Dad read the story books he gave me and I put on my new pyjamas and we had supper and it was time to go to bed and Dad said. . .

. . . "Will you give Annie a kiss?" and I said, "No, I can't, she's a wicked stepmother and a horrible witch!" and then I thought, Oh no! Now she'll turn me into a toad!

But she didn't.

She cried.

I felt bad.

So I put my arms around her and kissed her better, and she smiled and hugged me,

and I cried and Dad cried, and we all cried and hugged each other.

Then Dad took me up to bed and told me a story about a fairy godmother.
And now I've discovered I must be a wizard —

because I used to have a wicked stepmother but I kissed her,
and now she's turned into a fairy godmother.